TALES FOR THE
PERFECT
CHILD

. . .

tales for the

child

by

FLORENCE PARRY HEIDE

pictures by

VICTORIA CHESS

BEECH TREE
NEW YORK

• • •

The Library of Congress has cataloged the Lothrop, Lee & Shepard edition
of *Tales for the Perfect Child* as follows:
Heide, Florence Parry. Tales for the perfect child.
Summary: Vignettes of children whose less than desirable behavior is masked in
insidious but acceptable ways.
ISBN 0-688-03892-1 (trade)
ISBN 0-688-03893-X (lib. bdg.)
1. Conduct of life—Juvenile fiction. 2. Children's stories, American.
[1. Conduct of life—Fiction. 2. Short stories.] I. Chess, Victoria, ill. II. Title.
PZ7.1136Tal 1985 [E] 84-5710

10 9 8 7 6 5 4 3 2 1
First Beech Tree Edition, 1999
ISBN 0-688-16673-3

These tales are dedicated to

perfect children,

everywhere

F. P. H. & V. C.

• • •

Contents

TALES FOR THE PERFECT CHILD

• • •

Ruby

Ruby wanted to go over to Ethel's house to play. But Ruby's mother said, "You have to watch Clyde."

Clyde was Ruby's baby brother. He had just learned to walk.

"I don't want to watch Clyde. I want to go over to Ethel's house to play," said Ruby.

Ruby's mother was tired. She had been watching
Clyde all day. "You have to watch Clyde because
I have to take a bubble bath," said Ruby's mother.
She went into the bathroom.

Ruby called Ethel. "I'll be over in a minute."

Then Ruby watched Clyde.

She watched him take all of the clothes out
of all of the drawers in all of the bureaus in all
of the rooms.

She watched him take all of the rice and all
of the flour and all of the salt and all of the
sugar and all of the coffee out of all of the
kitchen cupboards and spill it all on the nice
clean floor.

She watched him pull the tablecloth off
the kitchen table. The bananas that had been
on the table landed on Clyde's head.

Ruby watched Clyde start to cry very loud.

Her mother came out of the bathroom.
"What's going on?" she asked. "I told you to
watch Clyde."

"I was watching him," said Ruby truthfully.
"I was watching him the whole time."

• • •

In a few minutes Ruby was ringing Ethel's
doorbell. "I told you I'd be over in a minute,"
she said. "I just had to watch Clyde."

Arthur

Arthur liked to wear his old comfortable
clothes and his old comfortable sneakers. He
did not like to get dressed up. He did not like
to wear white shirts and nice suits, and he did
not like to wear any of the nice ties he had
gotten for his birthday.

. . .

"Arthur," said his mother, "we're going to visit Aunt Eunice. Put on your white shirt and your nice suit and your new tie and your nice new shiny shoes."

Arthur did not want to get dressed up. He did not want to visit Aunt Eunice. He wanted to stay home in his old clothes and watch his favorite program.

"I want to stay here in my old clothes and watch my favorite program," said Arthur.

"Well, you're going with me to see Aunt Eunice, and that's that. And you're going to get dressed up, and that's that."

Arthur's mother always wanted to tell Arthur what was what. That was very thoughtful. Mothers are thoughtful people.

"All right," said Arthur.

Arthur's mother was surprised. Usually Arthur argued. Arthur was very good at arguing.

Arthur put on his white shirt and his nice
new suit and the tie that Aunt Eunice had given
him for his last birthday. He put on the new
shiny shoes.

"Now you look like a little gentleman," said
his mother.

And he did. He looked like a little gentleman.

. . .

As soon as he was all dressed up, Arthur
went out to the kitchen. He opened the
refrigerator. He poured himself a nice big
glass of grape juice. Some of it got on his face,
but most of it got on his white shirt and the
pretty new suit and the tie that Aunt Eunice
had given him for his birthday.

• • •

Then he went out to the yard. In a few
minutes his nice shiny shoes were all muddy.

His mother was sad.

"Oh, dear," she said. "You've spoiled all your
nice clothes. You can't go to see Aunt Eunice
looking like that. You'll have to stay home."

• • •

So Arthur changed back into his blue jeans
and T-shirt and his old comfortable sneakers.
His mother went to see Aunt Eunice, and
Arthur had to stay home and watch his
favorite television program.

■ ■ ■

Gertrude

&

Gloria

Children should be helpful.

That's what Gertrude and Gloria's mother always said. And she was right, just as mothers always are: children *should* be helpful. They should help with the dishes, for instance. It isn't fair for mothers and fathers to do all the work.

"Help clear the table, dears," said Gertrude
and Gloria's mother after dinner.
They started to help.

• • •

Gertrude carried the dishes over to the kitchen sink very very carefully.

Gloria was not careful. She dropped the dishes and broke three plates. Her mother was not happy.

"Help dry the dishes, dears," said their mother. "And be sure to put them away where they belong." Mothers always like to have everything in the right place. That makes it easier to find things.

Gertrude dried the dishes very very carefully
and put them just where they belonged.

Gloria put the cups where the plates should
be, and the plates where the pans should be,
and she broke her mother's very best teacup.

Her mother was sad.
She said she would not let Gloria
help with the dishes anymore.

• • •

Since Gertrude had been so extremely careful and helpful and had done such a very good job, she got to help with the dishes the next day and every day after that.

Good for Gertrude.

• • •

Bertha

It was a lovely, cool, sunshiny day.

"It's a lovely, cool sunshiny day," said Bertha's mother. "Stop watching television and go outside and play."

Bertha did not want to go outside and play. She wanted to stay indoors and watch cartoons.

"Out you go," said Bertha's mother. "And don't argue."

Bertha wasn't going to try to argue anyway, because Bertha never won arguments with her mother. Mothers usually win arguments. Mothers are bigger than children.

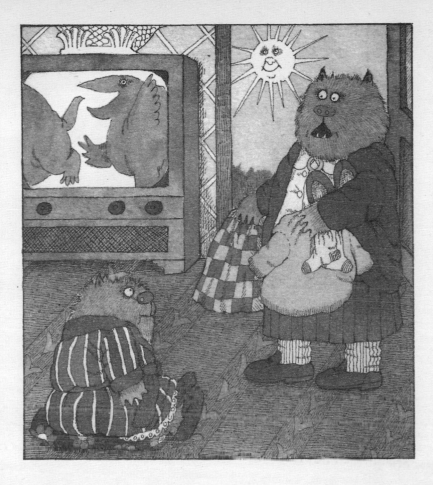

The cartoon was at a very exciting part.

"I'll go outside as soon as I get dressed," said Bertha.

"Well, hurry up," said Bertha's mother.

"I am hurrying," said Bertha.

■　■　■

45

That was not true. Bertha tried to move
very very slowly. It always took her an
extremely long time to get ready for anything,
especially when she was watching television.

"Hurry up, Bertha," said Bertha's mother.

Bertha had tied knots in her shoelaces so
that it would take a very long time to untie
them. While she untied the knots, she
watched the cartoon.

Bertha put on one shoe. She put the other
shoe in a big vase.

"I can't find my shoe," said Bertha.

"Of course you can," said Bertha's mother.
"I'll help you find it. It can't have walked off
by itself."

What she said was true: Bertha's shoe couldn't have walked off by itself. Bertha's mother had some very sensible sayings.

Bertha's mother looked and looked, but she could not find Bertha's shoe.

"Well, you can wear your old sneakers," she said finally. "Here they are. Hurry up and put them on."

"I can't find my jacket," said Bertha.

That was because Bertha had put her jacket in a very secret place.

Bertha's mother looked and looked for the jacket. By the time she found it, it had started to rain.

Bertha settled down in front of the
television set. It was a lovely, cool, rainy day.

Harriet

Harriet was a very good whiner. She practiced and practiced, and so of course she got better and better at it. Practice makes perfect.

Some children hardly ever whine. Can you believe that? So of course they never get to be very good at it.

"Can I have a piece of that blueberry pie?"
Harriet asked her mother while her mother
was fixing dinner.

Guests were coming, and her mother
wanted everything to be very nice.

"No, Harriet. The pie is for after dinner.
We're having roast beef."

Children like Harriet are not interested in
roast beef when they are interested in pie.

■ ■ ■

"I want a piece of pie," whined Harriet. She used her best whiny voice.

"I said no and I mean no," said Harriet's mother. She always liked to say what she meant.

Harriet's mother started to make some nice tomato aspic.

Harriet kept whining, "Can I have some pie, can I have some pie?"

Harriet's mother kept saying that when she said no she meant no. Harriet's mother tried to concentrate on the aspic, but that was very hard to do because Harriet was whining.

Good whiners make it very hard for anyone to think of anything else.

"Why don't you color in your nice new
coloring book?" asked Harriet's mother.

"I want some pie now," whined Harriet.

"Dinner will be ready pretty soon," said
Harriet's mother.

"But I want some pie now," whined Harriet.

A good whiner sticks to one subject. A good
whiner never gives up.

Harriet kept whining, and her mother kept trying to get dinner ready.

"I want some pie," whined Harriet, and her mother burned the gravy.

"All right, all right," her mother said. She was very tired of hearing Harriet whine.

Harriet stopped whining while she had her piece of pie. She always rested up between whines. That's what good whiners always do.

Irving

Irving was visiting his cousin Irma.

Irving did not like to visit Irma. The reason Irving did not like to visit Irma was because Irving did not like Irma. The reason Irving did not like Irma was because Irma always got her own way. The reason Irma always got her own way was because Irma's parents did not like Irma to cry and carry on. And Irma always cried and carried on when she didn't get her own way.

This Saturday afternoon Irma's parents
were planning to take Irma and Irving to a
lovely piano recital at Miss Meesley's house.
Irma was the kind of person who liked
piano recitals and concerts and educational
programs. Irving was the kind of person who
liked baseball and circuses and movies.

. . .

Before they left for the recital at Miss
Meesley's house, Irving said to Irma, "It's too
bad about the bats at Miss Meesley's."

"Bats?" asked Irma, and her eyes grew
unusually large. Usually her eyes were unusually
small. "What bats?" Irma was the kind of
person who was very very afraid of bats.

. . .

"I suppose your parents didn't want to tell
you," said Irving. "Miss Meesley has a problem
with bats this week. Swooping bats. They start
to swoop when they hear the music." Irving
never cared whether he told a lie or not.

• • •

68

"Besides, there's a very good movie," said
Irving. "There are no bats in the theater," he
added.

"Okay," said Irma. "We'll go to the movie
instead."

* * *

Irma's parents did not want to go to the
movie instead, but Irma cried and carried on,
and so she got her own way.

. . .

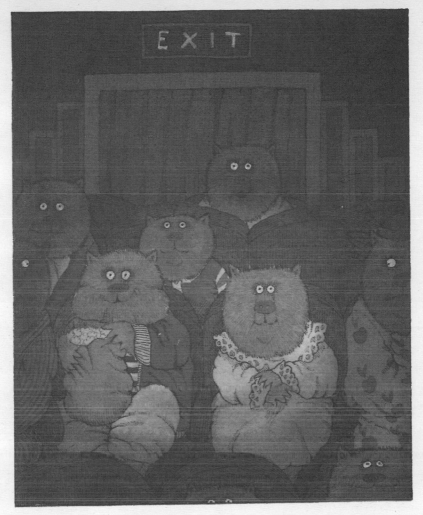

They all went to the movie instead of
the lovely piano recital.

Irving decided he probably liked Irma
better than he'd thought.

• • •

Ethel

Emma was kind.

Rose was helpful.

Gladys was very polite.

Harry was the kind of person who *shared*.

And Ethel was a perfect child. You don't meet many of those.

■ ■ ■

But then something terrible happened.
Ethel discovered bubble gum. Isn't that awful?
Of course Ethel's mother and father hated
bubble gum. All parents hate bubble gum,
and parents know best.

They didn't like the way Ethel chewed it,
they didn't like the way Ethel popped it,
they didn't like the way Ethel blew great big
beautiful bubbles with it, and they didn't like
the way it stuck to everything.

• • •

"We don't ever want to see you chewing
bubble gum again, Ethel," her parents told her.
And they never did.

. . .

That doesn't mean that Ethel stopped
chewing bubble gum. Oh, no. But her
parents never *saw* her chewing it.

That's another good thing about Ethel.
Ethel was a very sensible person.

· · ·